BROWNIE & PEARL
Get Dolled Up

by CYNTHIA RYLANT ❀ pictures by BRIAN BIGGS

Beach Lane Books
New York London Toronto Sydney

Brownie and Pearl
like to get dolled up.
What shall they wear?

Brownie finds feathers.

Pearl finds pearls.

A little powder?

Lipstick?

For Brownie.

Glitter?

See that kitty sparkle!

What about the hair?

Very shiny!

Now some rosy spray.

Time to go out.

"You are so dolled up!" everyone says.

Brownie and Pearl know it.

They are feathery.
They are powdery.
They sparkle.
They shine.

They were *so*
DOLLED UP!

For Elliot and her best friend, Emma
—B. B.

BEACH LANE BOOKS

An imprint of Simon & Schuster Children's Publishing Division

1230 Avenue of the Americas, New York, New York 10020

Text copyright © 2010 by Cynthia Rylant

Illustrations copyright © 2010 by Brian Biggs

BEACH LANE BOOKS is a trademark of Simon & Schuster, Inc.

For information about special discounts for bulk purchases, please contact Simon & Schuster

Special Sales at 1-866-506-1949 or business@simonandschuster.com.

The Simon & Schuster Speakers Bureau can bring authors to your live event.

For more information or to book an event, contact the Simon & Schuster Speakers Bureau

at 1-866-248-3049 or visit our website at www.simonspeakers.com.

Book design by Dan Potash and Sonia Chaghatzbanian

The text for this book is set in Berliner Grotesk.

The illustrations for this book are rendered digitally.

Manufactured in China

0614 SCP

4 6 8 10 9 7 5

Library of Congress Cataloging-in-Publication Data

Rylant, Cynthia.

Brownie & Pearl get dolled up / Cynthia Rylant ; illustrated by Brian Biggs.—1st ed.

p. cm.

Summary: After playing dress-up, a little girl and her cat show off their finery.

ISBN 978-1-4169-8631-7 (hardcover : alk. paper)

[1. Play—Fiction. 2. Cats—Fiction.] I. Biggs, Brian, ill. II. Title. III. Title: Brownie and Pearl get dolled up.

PZ7.R982Br 2010

[E]—dc22

2009019972